Imogene
the word machine.

Illustrated by
Robert Gibson

Written by
Judith W. Brown

Imogene Pendercot really loves words a lot!
I've heard it said, yes, I've been told
When Imogene was one day old,
Snuggled cozily in her bed,
She opened up her mouth and said:

Before she ever learned to walk,
Imogene knew how to talk!
It was really quite absurd
The way she spouted all those words.
So many words that wanted out,
That Imogene would up and shout:

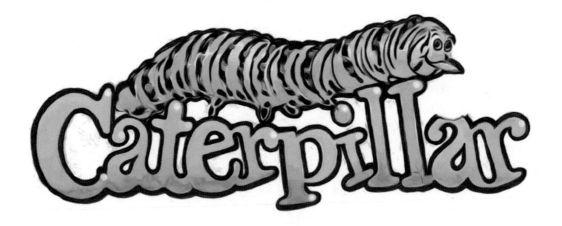

Lullaby
Curlicue
tiptoe
Toe Jam
Ticklish
Umbrella
Dazzling
Ripple
zero
Glitter

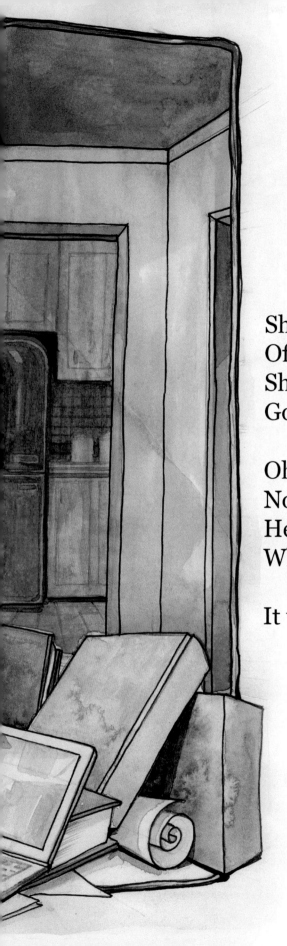

She kept a list, both great and small,
Of words she liked best of all.
She even wrote them on the wall.
Good thing she wasn't very tall.

Oh my goodness, Imogene.
Now you have a wall to clean!
Her list of words grew and grew.
What was Imogene to do?

It was a DILEMMA!

Imogene read every book
In every little bookstore nook.
Sometimes she would draw a crowd,
Because she loved to read aloud.
The words would dance upon her tongue,
And tumble out like they'd been sung.

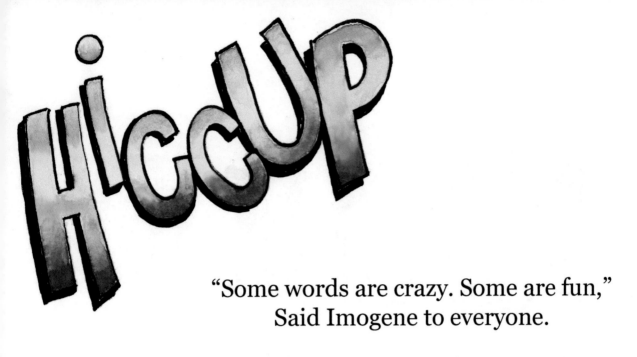

"Some words are crazy. Some are fun,"
Said Imogene to everyone.

KALEIDO

"Some words are long and hard to say,

Pheno

SCOPE

And twist your tongue in every way!"

menon

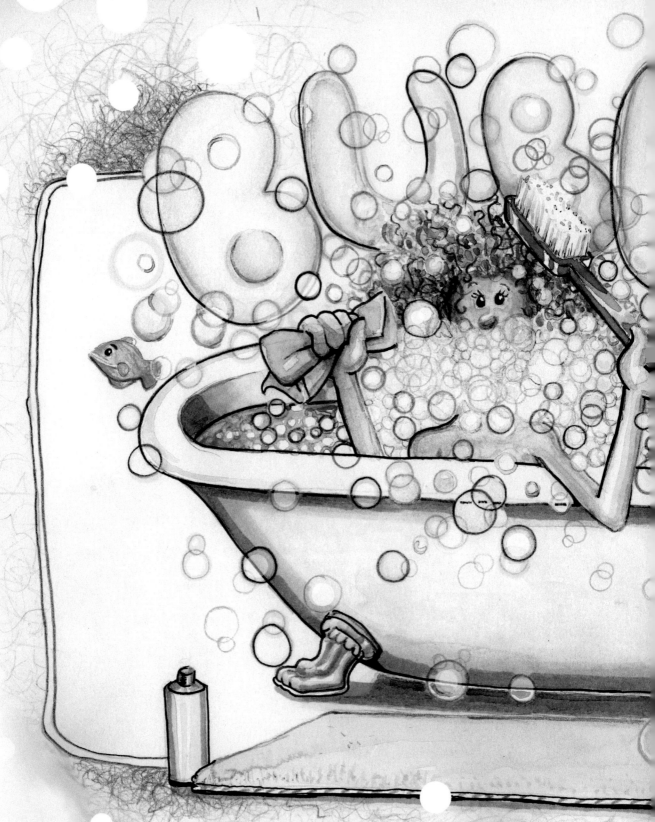

"Some in your mouth will bounce around,

Like a ball upon the ground."

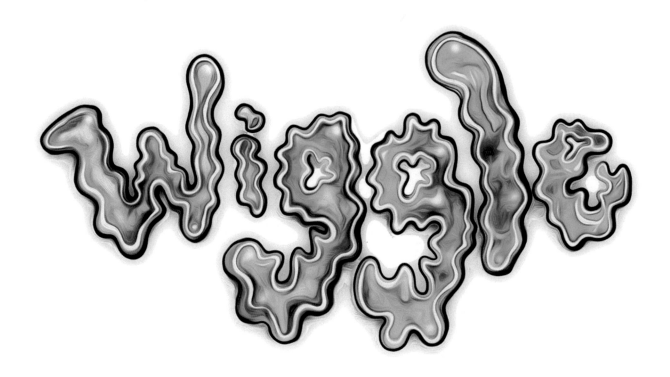

"Some words when said, I truly feel,
Are hard to say while sitting still."

Jiggle
fidgety

"Oh, my precious darling girl,
You put my mind in such a whirl,"
Said her mother to Imogene.
"Why you're a walking, talking word machine!"

What? A walking, talking word machine?
Such a compliment, thought Imogene.

"Why yes," said Imogene with glee,
"When I grow up I want to be
A writer of words for all to read,
A speaker of words for all to heed."

"Words, words, words, they are my fate.
How I love to ARTICULATE!"

"I will buy a van, **BIG** and GREEN
With a sign that reads: Here's Imogene:
A traveling vocabulary queen."

"I'll travel the globe, east to west,
From north to south, I'll do my best
To learn new words, to hear new sounds
'Till every single word is found."

Be on the lookout for Imogene
In her van that's **BIG** and GREEN.
(It will be awhile, you can bet,
For she has no driver's license yet.)

And one day she might write a book
That you might find in a bookstore nook.
A book about Imogene Pendercot,
Who really loves words a lot!

Do you have a word for Imogene?
A word that she has never seen?
A word that she has never found?
Oh my! If so, go write it down!

_____

_____

_____

_____

_____

_____

_____

_____

_____

_____

Glossary

A note from Imogene: I imagine that you love words just like I do. So I decided to provide you with a glossary. A glossary is a list at the back of a book explaining or defining difficult or unusual words. I do love unusual words, don't you? However, if the word you are looking for is not listed here, then please do what lovers of words do—look it up in the dictionary. Have fun!

Articulate: able to express ideas clearly and effectively in speech or writing

Bangle: a large stiff ring that is worn as jewelry around the arm, wrist or ankle.

Bobble: to move up and down quickly or repeatedly

Caterpillar: a small creature that is like a worm with many legs, and that changes to become a butterfly or a moth.

Chow Mein: a combination of meat, mushrooms and vegetables with fried noodles that is served in Chinese restaurants in the U.S.

Curlicue: a decoratively curved line or shape

Dainty: small and pretty

Dazzling: to greatly impress or surprise someone by being very attractive or exciting

Dilemma: a situation in which you have to make a difficult choice

Etiquette: the rules indicating the proper and polite way to behave

Exuberant: very lively, happy or energetic

Fidgety: moving a lot because of nervousness, boredom, etc.

Flapdoodle: foolish words or nonsense

Goose Bumps: small bumps on your skin that are caused by cold, fear or a sudden feeling of excitement

Jiggle: to move or causes something to move with quick, short movements up and down or side to side

Kaleidoscope: a changing pattern or scene

Melody: a series of musical notes that form the main part of a song or piece of music

Pizazz: a quality or style that is exciting and interesting

Rhapsody: a piece of music that is meant to express a lot of emotion

Symphony: a long piece of music that is performed by an orchestra

Tadpole: a small creature that becomes a frog or toad, that has a rounded body and a long tail and that lives in water.

Tenacious: not easily stopped

Toe Jam: any material that collects between the toes

Vocabulary: the words that make up a language

Whirligig: a child's toy that spins rapidly

Zigzag: a line that has a series of short, sharp turns or angles

www.dictionary.com
www.learnersdictionary.com
freedictionary.com

Made in the USA
Coppell, TX
01 March 2022

74271582R00019